THE LEGEND OF THE
PANDA

retold by

LINDA GRANFIELD

illustrated by

SONG NAN ZHANG

Peace

Linda Granfield

TUNDRA BOOKS

Published in Canada by Tundra Books, *McClelland & Stewart Young Readers*,
481 University Avenue, Toronto, Ontario M5G 2E9

Published in the United States by Tundra Books of Northern New York,
P.O. Box 1030, Plattsburgh, New York 12901

Library of Congress Catalog Number: 97-62238

Canadian Cataloguing in Publication Data

Granfield, Linda
    The legend of the panda

ISBN 0-88776-421-5

1. Giant panda – Folklore. 2. Folklore – China. I. Zhang Song Nan, 1942-   .
II. Title.

PS8563.R356L43 1998   j398.2'0951'04529789   C97-932509-9
PZ8.1.G73Le 1998

We acknowledge the support of the Canada Council for the Arts for our publishing program.

We acknowledge the financial support of the Government of Canada through the
Book Publishing Industry Development Program for our publishing activities.

Design by Kong Njo

Color separations by Rainbow Digicolor Inc., Toronto

Printed and bound in Canada

1 2 3 4 5 6   03 02 01 00 99 98

Dedication

For some wonderful men in my life: Jeffrey Canton, Robin Muller, and Ken Setterington, with thanks for their support and friendship.

L.G.

I would like to dedicate this book to all the people who are keeping up the fight for a greener world.

S.N.Z.

Acknowledgments

Gratitude and bear hugs to those who helped bring this book to life: Kathy Lowinger and the staff at Tundra Books; Song Nan Zhang, whose gift is rare indeed; Susan M. Woodward, Assistant Curator, Centre for Biodiversity & Conservation Biology – Mammals, at the Royal Ontario Museum, Toronto; and Cal, Devon, and Brian Smiley, who endured the pandemonium.

Long years ago, Dolma, a young shepherdess, lived with her sisters in the Wolong Valley, deep in the mountains of Sichuan province.

*E*ach day, Dolma led her small flock of sheep up the steep slopes of the nearby mountain. The rat-a-tat of woodpeckers echoed as Dolma and her companions traveled past frosty waterfalls and over moss-covered rocky paths to the fragrant meadows.

*W*hile the sheep grazed, Dolma collected herbs to make medicines for the villagers. She also gathered mountain blossoms - red and gold poppies, gentians as blue as the mists that veiled the mountaintops, and purple violets that lifted their tiny faces to the sunlight.

*O*n a morning when the air was sweet with spring, a young animal crept from the nearby evergreen forest. "Will you join our flock, little Beishung?" laughed Dolma.

By the trickling stream, the white cub nibbled tender shoots. His hunger satisfied, he frolicked among the sheep and lambs like a furry acrobat celebrating the end of the bitter winter. And each day thereafter, the white cub joined Dolma's flock to feed and play.

As she had so often, one day Dolma left her flock to gather herbs. Among the dewy grasses, she filled her basket and returned to the meadow. Dolma smiled to see her peaceful flock.

Suddenly, a snow leopard pounced from a tree. With teeth bared, he attacked the white cub. "Beishung!" cried Dolma, as the sheep fearfully bleated.

*T*he leopard's sharp claws tore at the helpless little Beishung. Yet Dolma, without a thought for her own safety, grabbed a stout branch and rushed forward to beat the leopard mightily.

The wounded cub withdrew weakly into the flock. The angry leopard, eager to claim a life, turned upon Dolma. Moments later, the shepherdess lay lifeless upon the trampled grass, the basket's blossoms and herbs strewn about her.

Great were the lamentations in the Wolong Valley when the people learned of Dolma's death. Heavy was the grief of all the Beishung. They knew of Dolma's kindness to the cub, and of the brave act that had saved him from the leopard's claws.

On the appointed day, the sorrowful villagers gathered with Dolma's heartbroken sisters to bury the shepherdess. Gray clouds hung heavily over the mountains as the white cub led the Beishung to join the funeral procession.

As the bamboo grasses rustled in damp winds, the mourners smeared themselves with ashes. The Beishung wiped their tear-filled eyes with sooty paws and hugged themselves as they wept. They covered their ears against the loud lamentations and, wherever the animals touched their snowy bodies with ash, the black soot stained forever the thick white fur.

Dolma's sisters, convinced they could not live without her, were determined to join her in death. As the sisters' cries reached the snow-capped mountaintops, the earth beneath their feet spoke to them with fierce rumblings, as if it, too, were mourning. The villagers fell back in awe as the earth suddenly split wide and received the four loving sisters. Where the meadow once lay rose a mountain of four peaks that reached beyond the clouds.

And this is exactly why to this day, the giant panda, the 'bamboo-eater,' wears the black marks of mourning in memory of the brave shepherdess, Dolma. His home and refuge is in the protective forests of Siguniang, the 'Mountain of the Four Sisters.'

The Giant Panda

Ailuropoda melanoleuca

⌣.

Panda is a Nepalese word meaning 'bamboo-eater.' Giant panda fossils found in Asia reveal that the mammal appeared nearly two million years ago. Treasured as a palace pet by China's early emperors, the panda was believed to have the power to prevent disease, drive away evil spirits, and ward off natural disasters. It was also considered a symbol of strength and courage.

The western world first learned of the panda in 1869 when Père Armand David, a French missionary, sent a pelt to the Museum of Natural History in Paris. In 1928, United States President Teddy Roosevelt and his sons hunted for pandas in China and sent them home stuffed.

The first live panda seen outside China was Su-Lin who was shipped to the United States in 1936. Until she died after fourteen months, Su-Lin was exhibited at the Brookfield Zoo in Chicago - and there was panda-mania as photographs, toys, even bathing suits spread the image of the panda around the western world.

Pandas belong to their own subfamily within the bear family. The proper species name, *Ailuropoda melanoleuca*, means 'panda foot' (genus) 'black white' (species). In China, the panda is called *daxiong mao*, meaning 'large bear cat.'

The panda has the digestive system of a carnivore, or meat-eater; however, through the centuries, it has adapted to a vegetarian diet and feeds mainly on the leaves and stems of bamboo. In fact, the panda spends most of its waking hours eating up to forty pounds of bamboo each day. Its flexible forepaws allow the panda to hold onto its food. Strong flattened molars and powerful jaw muscles enable the panda to crush tough bamboo stalks, and a thick lining protects the panda's esophagus from bamboo splinters.

The giant panda has thick, coarse fur that protects it from the cool, damp climate of the Chinese forests. Some scientists believe that the panda's black markings provide camouflage in the shadows of the forests; others think the coloring warns other animals to keep away from the panda's territory.

The panda leads a solitary life of eating and sleeping, except in the spring when mating may occur. One or two tiny cubs, covered in fine white fur, are born in August or September. After one month, they develop their black panda markings. The young live with their mother until they're about eighteen months old. Then the pandas are on their own as the mother leaves to breed once again.

Scientists estimate that fewer than one thousand pandas remain living in the wild in China today. As people develop more land, the bamboo groves are destroyed and the panda has less to eat, and a smaller area to inhabit. Climate changes and the natural life cycle of the bamboo in some areas have left the panda with little to eat. Despite strict laws, hunters continue to trap and kill the panda as its pelt becomes increasingly valuable.

Efforts to save the endangered panda – the international symbol for the World Wildlife Fund – have been well-documented. The WWF is an agency that has been working on panda conservation in China since 1980. A captive breeding program at Wolong, China's largest panda reserve, has been successful in recent years: thirty-six cubs have been born since 1987, and twenty-one have survived past six months.

There are plans to create new reserves in China, and to establish links between isolated panda populations. Special programs continue to alert the world of the decreasing number of pandas, and recent technology provides more options in the fight to save the endangered panda. Because of the panda's low reproductive rate, Chinese scientists plan to produce the world's first test-tube panda early in the next century.